CAREERS ON THE FRONT LINE

NAVY CAREERS

CYNTHIA O'BRIEN

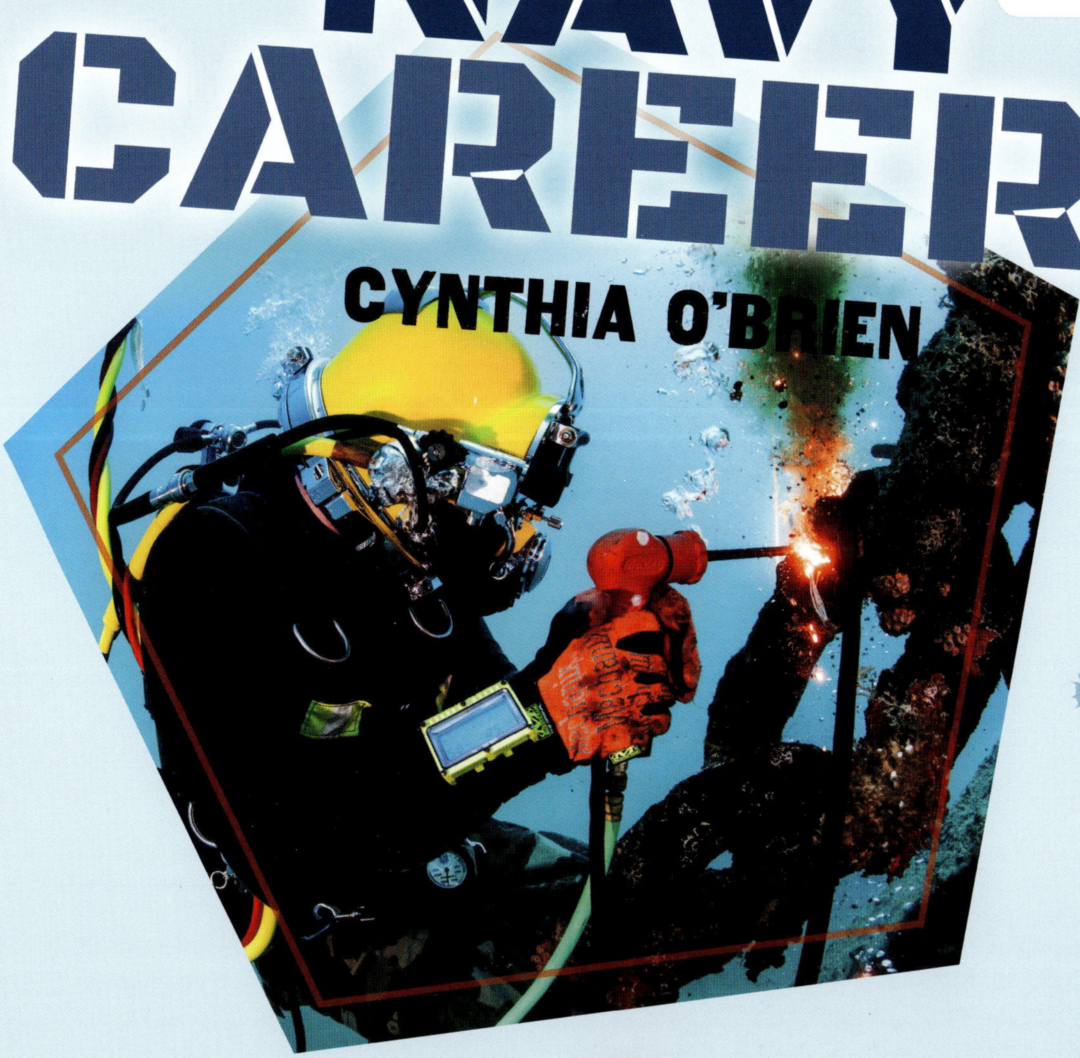

CRABTREE
PUBLISHING COMPANY
WWW.CRABTREEBOOKS.COM

CRABTREE
PUBLISHING COMPANY
WWW.CRABTREEBOOKS.COM

Author: Cynthia O'Brien
Editors: Sarah Eason
Jennifer Sanderson
Ellen Rodger
Proofreader: Tracey Kelly
Indexer: Tracey Kelly
Editorial director:
Kathy Middleton
Interior design: Emma DeBanks
Cover and logo design:
Katherine Berti
Photo research: Rachel Blount
Print coordinator:
Katherine Berti
Consultant: David Hawksett

Written, developed, and produced for Crabtree Publishing by Calcium Creative Ltd.

Photo Credits:
t=Top, tr=Top Right, tl=Top Left
Inside: Defense Logistics Agency: U.S. Marine Corps photo by Cpl. Daisha R. Johnson: p. 23; Department of Defense: U.S. Navy photo by Mass Communication Specialist 1st Class Arthurgwain L. Marquez: pp. 1, 17; Midshipman 3rd Class Dominic Montez, U.S. Navy: p. 7; DVIDS: U.S. Navy photo by Mass Communication Specialist 3rd Class Danielle A. Baker: p. 8; U.S. Navy photo by Mass Communication Specialist 1st Class Kevin A. Flinn: p. 27; U.S. Navy photo by Chief Mass Communication Specialist Matthew R. White: p. 16; Shutterstock: Jason and Bonnie Grower: p. 28t; Vladimir Melnik: p. 28b; Anurake Singto-on: p. 29; U.S. Defense Story: U.S. Navy photo by Mass Communication Specialist 1st Class Fred Gray IV: p. 24; U.S. Marine Corps Forces Reserves: Pfc. Leslie Alcaraz: pp. 1, 21; Wikimedia Commons: Bundeswehr-Fotos: p. 19; MC3 Kristina D. Walton: p. 6; U.S. Marine Corps photo by Lance Cpl. Immanuel Johnson: p. 20; U.S. Navy photo by Mass Communication Specialist 1st Class Michael Billings: p. 13; U.S. Navy photo by Photographer's Mate 2nd Class Roadell Hickman: pp. 14–15; U.S. Navy photo by Mass Communication Specialist 2nd Class Jennifer S. Kimball: p. 25; U.S. Navy photo by Mass Communication Specialist 1st Class Andrew McCord: p. 9; U.S. Navy photo by Mass Communication Specialist 3rd Class Danna M. Morris: p. 12; U.S. Navy photo by Mass Communication Specialist Seaman Charles Oki: p. 11; U.S. Navy photo by Mass Communication Specialist 1st Class Jeremy Starr: p. 5; U.S. Navy photo by Chief Mass Communication Specialist Kathryn Whittenberger: p. 4. Front cover: Shutterstock

Library and Archives Canada Cataloguing in Publication

Title: Navy careers / Cynthia O'Brien.
Names: O'Brien, Cynthia (Cynthia J.), author.
Description: Series statement: Careers on the front line | Includes bibliographical references and index.
Identifiers: Canadiana (print) 20200283898 | Canadiana (ebook) 20200283901 | ISBN 9780778781400 (hardcover) | ISBN 9780778781462 (softcover) | ISBN 9781427125804 (HTML)
Subjects: LCSH: United States. Navy—Vocational guidance—Juvenile literature. | LCSH: United States. Navy—Recruiting, enlistment, etc.—Juvenile literature. | LCSH: Canada. Royal Canadian Navy—Vocational guidance—Juvenile literature. | LCSH: Canada. Royal Canadian Navy—Recruiting, enlistment, etc.—Juvenile literature.
Classification: LCC VB259 .O27 2020 | DDC j359.0023—dc23

Library of Congress Cataloging-in-Publication Data

Names: O'Brien, Cynthia (Cynthia J.) author.
Title: Navy careers / Cynthia O'Brien.
Description: New York : Crabtree Publishing Company, [2021] | Series: Careers on the front line | Includes index.
Identifiers: LCCN 2020029713 (print) | LCCN 2020029714 (ebook) | ISBN 9780778781400 (hardcover) | ISBN 9780778781462 (paperback) | ISBN 9781427125804 (ebook)
Subjects: LCSH: United States. Navy--Vocational guidance--Juvenile literature. | United States. Navy--Juvenile literature.
Classification: LCC VB259 .O27 2021 (print) | LCC VB259 (ebook) | DDC 359.0023/73--dc23
LC record available at https://lccn.loc.gov/2020029713
LC ebook record available at https://lccn.loc.gov/2020029714

Crabtree Publishing Company
www.crabtreebooks.com 1-800-387-7650

Printed in the U.S.A./082020/CG20200710

Published in Canada
Crabtree Publishing
616 Welland Ave.
St. Catharines, Ontario
L2M 5V6

Published in the United States
Crabtree Publishing
347 Fifth Ave
Suite 1402-145
New York, NY 10016

Published in the United Kingdom
Crabtree Publishing
Maritime House
Basin Road North, Hove
BN41 1WR

Published in Australia
Crabtree Publishing
3 Charles Street
Coburg North
VIC, 3058

CONTENTS

DEFENSE AT SEA

The navy is a vital branch of a country's military, or armed forces. The military protects and defends its country during war and in peacetime. Naval forces do this on and under oceans, seas, lakes, and rivers. The navy works with other branches of the military, such as the army and air force. Today, the United States Navy is the second largest in the world after China's. The Canadian Navy is much smaller, but it has the job of defending the world's longest coastline.

FIT FOR THE JOB

A career in the navy is much more complicated than simply spending time on or in the water. There are many different jobs sailors can do. **Enlisting** in the navy takes dedication, good physical fitness, and a willingness to travel. Sailors may be far away from home for long periods of time. The U.S. Navy, for example, has **bases** around the world and operates its **fleets** of watercraft in international ocean waters. Naval forces also protect the seas so that other sea traffic, such as cargo ships, can sail safely.

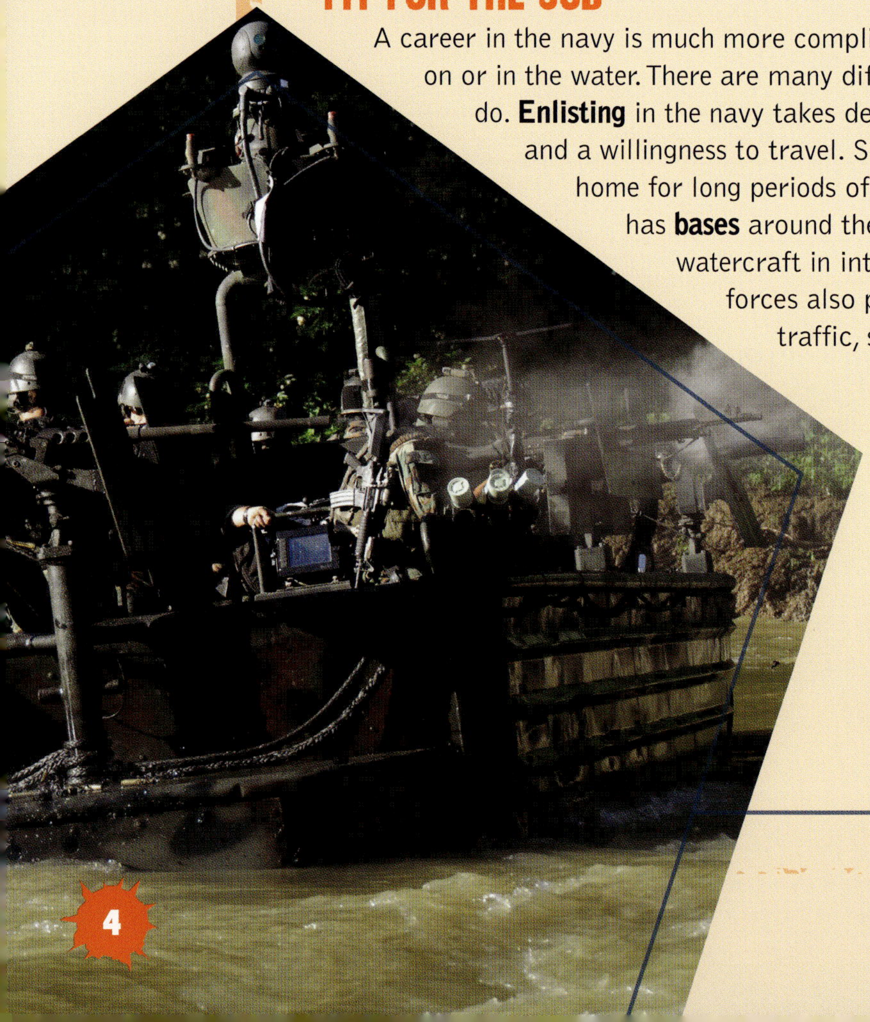

Naval vessels, such as this special operations craft, transport people and arms, or weapons. During peacetime, the navy patrols the seas and inland waters.

Enlisted sailors wear white dress uniforms for official functions.

JOINING THE NAVY

The U.S. Navy's core **values** are honor, courage, and commitment. The service expects sailors to uphold these values in all situations. After joining the Navy, new recruits have the benefits of learning new skills through classes and getting on-the-job training. They learn leadership skills and how to work as part of a team. Through experience and examples from their commanders, sailors also become skilled at handling different tasks at the same time. At all times, sailors have to be ready for emergency situations, from warfare to **natural disasters**.

Your FRONTLINE Career

Look for "Your Frontline Career" boxes. They highlight the skills and strengths needed for specific Navy careers. They can be used to help you decide whether a career in the Navy is for you and what roles might suit you best.

A FRONTLINE CAREER

There are two main paths to take when joining the U.S. Navy. One is to enlist, and the other is to be **commissioned** as an officer. Enlisted sailors make up most of the Navy's workforce. These sailors are specially trained to do one of hundreds of Navy jobs, from operating **radar** systems to working on engines. Enlisted sailors can also be cooks, medical aids, and **intelligence** specialists. Commissioned officers lead teams and operations. Their roles include naval operations managers, doctors, and engineers.

PATHS TO SUCCESS

The route to enlisting starts with a high school diploma and a test. U.S. citizens must take the Armed Service Vocational **Aptitude** Battery (ASVAB). To join the Canadian Navy, applicants take the Canadian Forces Aptitude Test (CFAT). Both tests give **recruiters** an idea of applicants' skills and where they should be placed. Officers must have a college or university degree and pass an officer aptitude test.

During training, sailors learn to fire weapons. They keep their skills sharp with regular exercises at sea.

Training includes challenges such as obstacle courses. This teaches sailors to work as part of a team.

IN AT THE DEEP END

Training for enlisted sailors starts after the first tests are passed. The Navy's **boot camp** is eight weeks long. Recruits also have to complete medical and dental examinations to make sure they are fit and healthy. They attend classes, undergo tough physical exercises, and learn how to deal with emergency situations. Learning is hands-on, and recruits take on many challenges, including active firearms training and firefighting, as part of their education.

BECOMING AN OFFICER

There are different routes to becoming an officer in the U.S. Navy. For those who already have a degree, Officer Candidate School is the main pathway. People may also choose to do reserve training (see below) or attend a naval college. To attend the U.S. Naval Academy, students need a nomination from a U.S. Senator or Representative, the U.S. President or Vice President, or the Secretary of the Navy. Senior enlisted sailors may apply for an officer commission, while a professional civilian, or ordinary person, may get a direct commission. In Canada, Naval Warfare Officers must receive specialized training at the Naval Officer Training Centre, a naval school in British Columbia.

ACTIVE DUTY OR RESERVE?

*Being an active duty sailor means a commitment to the Navy for at least two years. Others choose to become reserves. This is like a part-time job with the Navy. Reserves also pursue other civilian activities, such as continuing education or working in a job outside the Navy. Reserves can be **deployed** to active duty if needed.*

LEADING FROM THE FRONT

In the U.S. Navy, officers have ranks. These are positions that go from an ensign, a starting level of O-1, and upward. A commander is a O-5, while a captain is a O-6. A Canadian Navy captain has the rank of OF-5. A rank of captain, which takes at least nine years to achieve, is the most senior officer level under the Rear Admiral.

PUTTING IN THE WORK

After commission, an officer spends three years rising to the rank of lieutenant. Next, a lieutenant could be promoted to lieutenant commander and spend two years at that level. Finally, there are another three years of service as a commander. At this point, the Navy may promote a commander to captain. The Captain's Promotion Board makes the final decision on this promotion. The board bases their decision on years of service and an officer's job performance.

LIFE OF A CAPTAIN

Captains make life-and-death decisions aboard a ship. They command top secret operations and oversee hundreds of enlisted sailors and other officers. It takes experience, intelligence, and excellent leadership skills. In the U.S. Navy, there are more than 55,000 officers and just over 3,000 captains. Captains who prove themselves on the job may go on to the admiral ranks and oversee fleets.

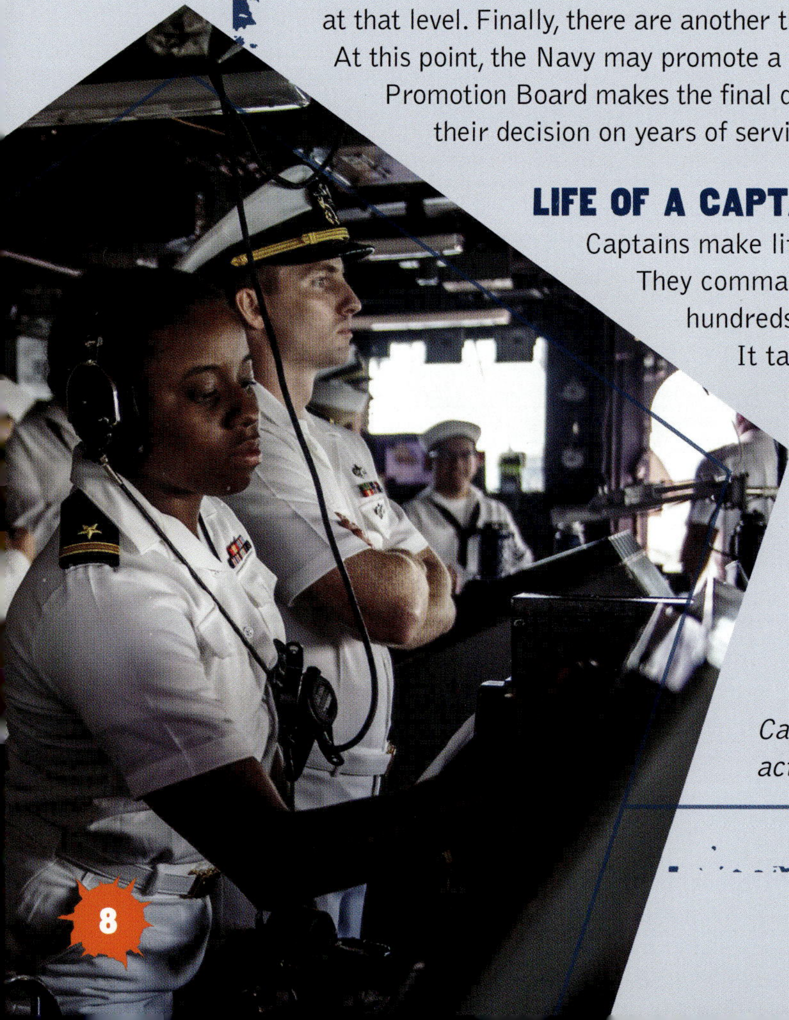

Captains are responsible for all activities and people on navy ships.

The rear admiral aboard the flagship, or leading ship, must keep in touch with the captains of all the ships.

TAKING CONTROL

Captains are in charge of ships such as aircraft carriers, assault vessels, destroyers, and submarines. To captain a warship that is not a submarine, an officer must complete the Surface Warfare Officer's course. Officers train aboard navy ships and learn about weapons systems, communications, ship handling, and more. A captain also needs to understand the workings of all the ship's departments, from deck operations to engineering. Captains on submarines need specialized training in undersea warfare.

WHAT IT TAKES TO LEAD

It takes intense training to command a ship. Leaders also have to be able to use all the technology on board. For example, captains have to know how to launch ***cruise missiles*** *and understand the ship's computers. They also have to understand how to lead a large crew. An aircraft carrier, for example, can have 5,000 crew on board.*

OFFICER Stories

Hung Ba Le:

REFUGEE TO COMMANDER

In 1975, the North Vietnamese seized, or took control, of the city of Saigon. This marked the end of the Vietnam War. It also forced thousands of South Vietnamese to flee the country, including Hung Ba Le and his family. Le was just five years old. He and his family joined hundreds of other refugees on an overcrowded fishing boat. The refugees were hungry and exhausted. Two days later, a U.S. Navy ship rescued them.

Your FRONTLINE Career

Is Being a Captain for You?

Sounds Great

- Traveling around the world and seeing new places
- Being in charge of a ship
- Being involved in top-level decisions
- Leading special missions

Things to Think About

- Responsible for hundreds of crew
- Must be able to make quick decisions under pressure
- Not so involved in hands-on work, which many people enjoy
- It takes a lot of training and many years to reach the rank of Captain

The Navy ship took the Le family to a U.S. base in the Philippines. From there, they traveled to a refugee camp in California. Finally, they settled in Virginia. It took eight years for the Le family to become U.S. citizens. In Vietnam, Le's father, Thong Ba Le, was a commander in the South Vietnamese Navy, and it was Le's dream to become a naval officer like his father. His hard work in high school paid off, and he gained a place at the United States Naval Academy. In 1992, Le graduated with a degree in economics. He went on to earn a master's degree in operations and a master's in business administration.

Le's education and training allowed him to hold many positions in the Navy, including auxiliaries officer, weapons officer, and combat services officer. He has worked on ships and with crews that have earned six Battle Excellence awards. In April 2009, Le's dream came true. He became commander of the USS *Lassen*. The ship is a destroyer in the U.S. 7th Fleet. The 7th Fleet includes as many as 80 ships and submarines, as well as 140 aircraft patrol. It protects about 48 million square miles (124.3 million sq km) of the Pacific and Indian Oceans.

Le commanded the USS Lassen *until December 2010. In 2018, he became the deputy director of Joint and Fleet Operations. In this role, he leads more than 100 active duty officers.*

Le was the first Vietnamese-American to become a U.S. Navy commander and then captain. During his first year as a commanding officer, Le led a mission to follow and observe a North Korean ship. The ship was thought to be carrying illegal weapons. Le and his crew forced the ship back to shore. In November 2009, Le returned to visit Vietnam for the first time in 35 years. That same month, the Navy awarded the Golden Anchor, now the Retention award, to the USS *Lassen*. This award goes to ships whose captain shows his support for the careers of his or her crew. It also recognizes the crew's loyalty to the captain.

BELOW THE WAVES

Submariners are part of the Navy's "silent service." They work on submarines, the vessels that defend and attack under the surface of the ocean. U.S. Navy submarines patrol the oceans around the country but can cross into international waters for defense, attack, and intelligence missions.

SUPER SUBS

The U.S. Navy has one of the largest fleets of submarines in the world. Attack submarines are the smallest, but they are very fast. They carry **torpedoes**. **Guided missile** submarines and **ballistic missile** submarines are larger and carry powerful missiles. All U.S. Navy submarines are **nuclear powered**. This makes them fast and quiet, and they do not have to come to the surface often. They can travel long distances, attack enemy ships on the surface, and destroy enemy submarines. The latest submarines come equipped with advanced **navigation** technology and **sonar**. They can also operate in polar regions and perform land attacks.

Sonar technicians detect things in the water and help navigate the submarine safely.

EARNING THEIR DOLPHINS

Submariners need to understand all the sub's systems to earn their dolphins, or to qualify as a submariner. Submariners start their careers in the same way as other sailors with the same basic training. After training, sailors volunteer to be submariners. The Navy then considers these volunteers after they pass mental and physical tests. Then the volunteers go through months of training. Officers and some crew must also have nuclear power training. Submarine officers oversee operations such as gathering information and shooting weapons. The crew operates the equipment, such as sonar, and makes repairs. During training, submarine crew learn about this equipment. They also learn how to handle emergency situations, such as fire and flooding.

BRAVING THE DEEP

Being on a submarine has to be one of the toughest jobs in the Navy. It takes special training, determination, and focus to serve on a submarine. The crew has shifts of work to keep the submarine running all the time. They keep watch for an 8-hour shift and then have 16 hours to do other work. Being on watch means doing a submariner's job, such as radio operator. The other hours include taking some time to sleep before the next watch begins.

Submariners deal with all water leaks, but a flood is an emergency. They must get to the submarine's escape chamber to survive.

SUBMARINE Stories

Mission 7:

SPY SUB

For two months in early 2013, the USS *Jimmy Carter* disappeared from view. Then in March, the attack submarine turned up damaged in Pearl Harbor, Hawaii. We know little about what caused the damage, but we have some clues. The first clue is that the **covert** mission earned the unit, or crew, a Presidential Unit Citation. This is a high honor awarded to military units that have shown "extraordinary heroism against an armed enemy." Also, the USS *Jimmy Carter* is no ordinary submarine. The U.S. Navy built this nuclear-powered armed vessel for dangerous, secret missions. It is the ultimate spy sub.

Your FRONTLINE Career

Is Being a Submariner for You?

Sounds Great

- Be involved in secret missions
- Be part of a close team
- Have a highly regarded role in the Navy and be paid well
- Travel all over the world

Things to Think About

- Being in small spaces with a lot of people for a long time
- Very little privacy
- No windows or sunlight
- Living in an underwater vessel for two or three months at a time. Submariners in an attack sub may stay underwater even longer

Who was the armed enemy that the USS *Jimmy Carter* encountered? Even today, the crew of the USS *Jimmy Carter* is not allowed to talk about it. Also, Mission 7 and others may involve special units, such as Navy SEALs, since the sub has room to carry about 50 extra people. They, too, have to keep silent. We do know that the USS *Jimmy Carter* carries nuclear weapons, such as tomahawk missiles, so the crew is trained to maintain and operate these weapons.

The Navy uses subs such as the USS *Jimmy Carter* for intelligence and **reconnaissance** operations. The $3 billion sub was the last Seawolf-class fast attack vessel built. It was made for **stealth**, so it is very quiet and very fast. It can also dive at least 800 feet (244 m) into the ocean and stay there for six months. The crew controls unmanned underwater vehicles (UUVs) and remotely operated vehicles (ROVs). These tools can find and tap into underwater cable used for the Internet. They can place tracking sensors to locate and identify foreign submarines. Meanwhile, the crew records sounds and takes photographs of whatever it can.

In 2017, the USS *Jimmy Carter* appeared again after another mystery mission. This time, the crew flew the Jolly Roger flag. It is Navy tradition to fly the black-and-white flag after a successful mission. But we may never know what this operation was about. Only the crew and top navy officers know...

The crew of the USS Jimmy Carter *spends most of the time at sea on secret* ***surveillance*** *or other missions. They return to shore for leave and training.*

DIVING DEEP

Imagine diving into icy Arctic water to repair a ship or diving in a classified underwater operation. This is the life of Navy divers. The U.S. Navy divers' motto, "We Dive the World Over," reflects their willingness to go anywhere and take on any mission. Navy divers are part of the Naval Special Operations unit, and the Navy depends on them for many different tasks. They scour the seabed in submarines for mines. They do repairs on ship hulls and replace heavy propellers. Divers go deep under the sea to recover sunken vessels, aircraft, or parts. They also back up other military teams such as the Marines.

DANGER BELOW

The Navy calls on its divers when any missions or operations need people underwater. Navy divers are search-and-rescue experts. When disasters strike, Navy divers are on hand. They go on submarine rescue missions and look for **debris** when airplanes go down in the sea. Rescue and **salvage** operations may take the submarine 850 feet (259 m) below the surface. Navy divers also help keep ports and harbors safe by inspecting jetties and ship hulls and checking for threats, such as underwater explosives.

UNDERWATER MEDICS

Diving medical technicians (DMTs) are trained Navy divers with a difference. They have extra training to deal with diver injuries and illnesses. One of the main issues they deal with is decompression sickness, or "the bends." This happens when divers come up to the surface too quickly and when there is a sudden change in air or water pressure. Divers with the bends suffer severe pain in their joints and bones. DMTs are there to help.

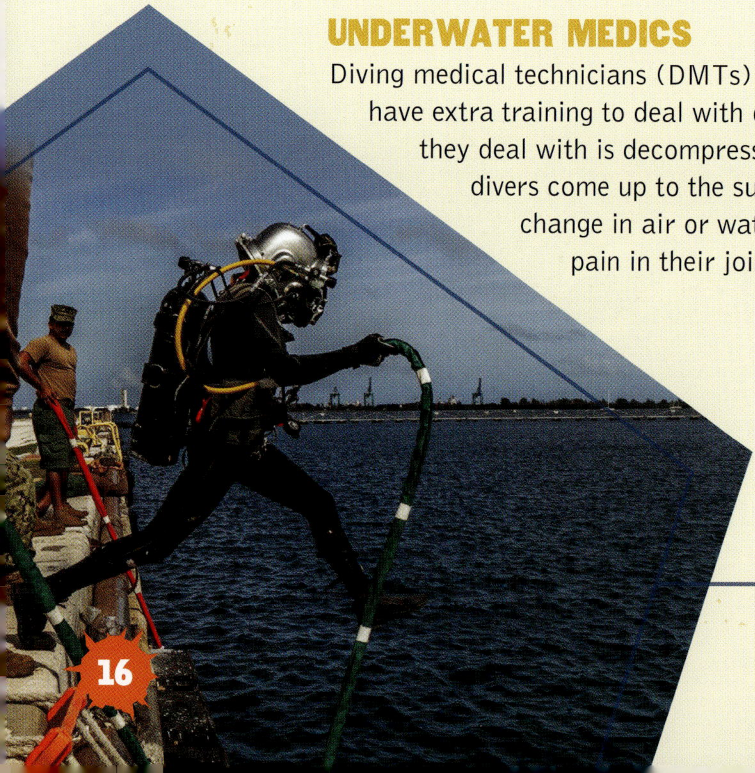

Seabee divers are the Navy's underwater construction workers. Their duties include constructing, maintaining, and repairing bridges and piers, or areas where ships dock.

Navy divers use special underwater cutting and welding tools to repair ships and submarines.

EXPERIMENTAL DIVING UNIT

Some Navy divers work with scientists, engineers, technicians, and others in the Experimental Diving Unit (EDU). The U.S. Navy has a large ocean ***simulation*** *chamber and three other chambers with different temperatures and depths. Navy divers take part in experiments in the ocean simulator. They test new equipment in different scenarios to make sure it is safe and effective.*

TOUGH TRAINING

U.S. Navy divers must be super fit. The diving program accepts people under 30 years old only. Specialist diver training schools take students through difficult physical tests. After seven weeks of this testing, divers have 15 more weeks of training. They learn about maintaining and repairing ships and how to use underwater tools. Then it is time for the real thing. During fleet training, divers use scuba equipment. Scuba equipment helps them breathe underwater, so they can stay underwater for much longer using this equipment. They also learn how to use surface supplied air and mixed gas systems. These systems link divers to the ship by tubes. They get air through there but also communications and electricity to power underwater lights. Skilled divers can go on to become First Class or Master Divers.

DIVER Stories

Commander Leanne Crowe:

DANGER IN THE DESERT

The desert does not seem like the most obvious place to find a Navy diver, but clearance divers form a specialized unit. These divers train for two years for a very dangerous job. They find, identify, and dispose of explosives in the water or on land. In particular, clearance divers are specially trained to find improvised explosive devices (IEDs). IEDs can be hidden anywhere. Commander Leanne Crowe was the first female clearance diver in the Canadian Navy.

Crowe was commanding a diving unit in Canada when she was deployed to Afghanistan. She became one of more than 40,000 Canadians who served in the **Afghanistan War** from 2001 to 2014. The Canadians joined the United States and other **allied** forces. The long, deadly conflict was made much worse by IEDs. IEDs are cheap and quick to make. The enemy forces in Afghanistan hid them everywhere. Clearance divers such as Crowe had to find them before they exploded. The divers wear heavy bomb suits for protection. This was hot, sweaty work in Afghanistan because temperatures in the desert can soar to more than 122 degrees Fahrenheit (50 degrees C). The heat did not stop Crowe. Not only did she have to find the bombs, she also had to find out who was building them. She needed to stop the bomb makers from getting the money and the materials to make the bombs. This quickly became Crowe's number one priority.

Your FRONTLINE Career

Is Being a Diver for You?

Sounds Great

- Choice of different roles, including construction
- Days are not routine
- Travel all over the world and diving in different seas
- Learning and using the latest equipment and diving techniques

Things to Think About

- Working underwater a lot of the time
- Relying on equipment for breathing
- Working in tight spaces
- Work can be in very dangerous conditions, especially if working with IEDs

Clearance divers in the U.S. Navy are called Explosive Ordnance Disposal Technicians. In both the U.S. and Canadian navies, people are trained in chemical, ***biological****, and nuclear bombs. Their heavy bomb suits and helmets help protect them in the event of a blast.*

Some of the bomb makers used the material in **fertilizers** to make IEDs. Crowe worked to keep this material from entering the country. She taught the border police what to look for and how to get rid of the material safely. She also developed a course to teach people how to avoid IEDs. Today, Crowe works at the Canadian Forces College, a military school for officer training.

THE MARINES

Marines are highly specialized combat sailors who work on the sea, on land, and in the air. There are more than 185,000 U.S. Marines on active duty. Many thousands are stationed around the world, so they are ready to go wherever they are needed. Marine units are deployed on U.S. Navy ships as necessary.

DUTY CALLS

Marines provide extra **security** and direct firepower to enemy shores. They are highly skilled fighters, and their missions are some of the most dangerous in the military. When a hurricane or other natural disaster strikes, Marines are there for rescue and relief operations. Marines also protect U.S. embassies in other countries. The Department of the Navy oversees the Marine Corps, but the force is a separate unit.

SEA TO LAND COMBAT

Marines are often the first military force to arrive on the scene, so they must come prepared to leap into combat. Marines are also experts in **amphibious** warfare. As part of the **infantry** unit, marines operate Amphibious Assault Vehicles or Amphibious Combat Vehicles. These armored vehicles come equipped with machine guns and other weapons. Marines are trained to use the vehicles to launch attacks from the sea and to invade enemy shores quickly. This way, they can secure the site ahead of other forces, such as the Army. They also use the vehicles to approach sites that may be suitable for military bases.

The new Amphibious Combat Vehicle is superfast and mobile on land. It carries more marines and weapons, getting them quickly on land and ready for combat.

Marines take part in tactical defense and movement under fire training to prepare them for action.

WOMEN IN THE MARINES

Women have been part of the Marine Corps since 1918. In 1993, the first women flew combat aircraft. By 2016, women could serve in all combat positions. In 2018, 100 years after the first female Marines joined, Lieutenant Marina Hierl became the first woman to lead an infantry platoon. Today, there are still fewer women in the Marines than in other military services.

BECOMING A MARINE

It takes fierce willpower to be part of the Marine Corps. People can enlist at 17 years old with a high school diploma. Then there are 13 weeks of intense physical training. Even after Marines graduate this boot camp, they must pass physical and combat fitness tests every year. The testing includes running 3 miles (4.8 km) in under 28 minutes for the youngest men or 31 minutes for the youngest women. Marines do sprint tests to make sure they can move quickly in battles. Another part of the combat test covers things Marines might face in battle. This is a quick-moving test that includes reloading ammunition, crawling along the ground, and carrying another Marine to safety.

MARINE Stories

John L. Canley: MEDAL OF HONOR

The Vietnam War had been raging since 1955. In 1965, 3,500 Marines were the first U.S. forces to arrive in South Vietnam. Three years later, Marine Gunnery Sergeant John L. Canley fought in one of the fiercest battles of the war. Just after midnight on January 30, 1968, the North Vietnamese Army (NVA) and the Viet Cong began a series of deadly attacks on towns and cities in South Vietnam. The attacks became known as the Tet Offensive.

Your FRONTLINE Career

Is Being a Marine for You?

Sounds Great

- Action-packed career
- Deployed all over the world
- Considered an elite, or special, division of the Navy
- Smaller division means close bonds with fellow marines

Things to Think About

- Often first on the front line in dangerous situations, including natural disasters
- Long tours of duty mean being far away from family for long periods of time
- One of the toughest, longest boot camps

On January 31, NVA troops seized control of Hue, an ancient Vietnamese city. At the time, Canley was part of the Alpha Company, First Battalion, First Marines. When the NVA and Viet Cong began their **siege**, the Alpha Company received their orders. They were to free Hue.

The thousands of enemy fighters far outnumbered the Alpha Company Marines, who were just 147. Canley and the others fought off enemy fire every step of the way. Canley braved the attacks to rescue injured Marines and carry them to safety. He saved the first fallen Marine as an enemy tank barreled toward him.

Then enemy fire wounded Alpha's commanding officer, so Canley took over.

One by one, the Marines cleared buildings of enemy soldiers. Gunfire met them at every turn. Bravely, Canley stood in the open to distract the Viet Cong inside a school building. As they began to fire at him, Marines attacked and took over the building. Canley then dropped an explosive that forced the enemy to retreat.

Canley was injured, but two days later, he and other Marines faced more fighting at a hospital compound. Twice, Canley risked his life to rescue wounded Marines. He scaled the hospital walls without any protection from enemy fire. The Battle of Hue continued for almost another 20 days. On February 25, South Vietnamese forces raised the national flag over Hue.

In 1970, Canley received the Navy Cross, the second-highest award for combat. In 2018, President Trump presented him with the Medal of Honor, the highest honor for valor against an enemy force. Canley was the 300th U.S. Marine to receive the medal. He had saved the lives of more than 20 Marines.

John L. Canley's name is in the Hall of Heroes. The Hall of Heroes is in the U.S. Defense headquarters, the Pentagon, and honors military heroes.

BEHIND THE FRONT LINE

There are thousands of people who support the Navy on the front line. These sailors may never see combat, though they may be very close to it. They are always crucial to successful missions wherever they are working. Medics, nurses, nuclear power technicians, and flight operations officers support frontline teams. The Navy also needs people to work on finance or legal affairs. Nuclear technicians make sure that submarines, aircraft carriers, and weapons systems work the way they should. Other sailors work to decode top secret intelligence.

COMMUNICATIONS AND INTELLIGENCE

Some of the most important work in the Navy involves information technology. Navy **cryptologic** technicians and intelligence specialists, for example, analyze information and prepare notes for officers. They also help track targets and work in **counterintelligence** by **intercepting** enemy communications. People in these jobs work with the most advanced computer systems, often on large ships. Intelligence work is crucial for defending a country from attack.

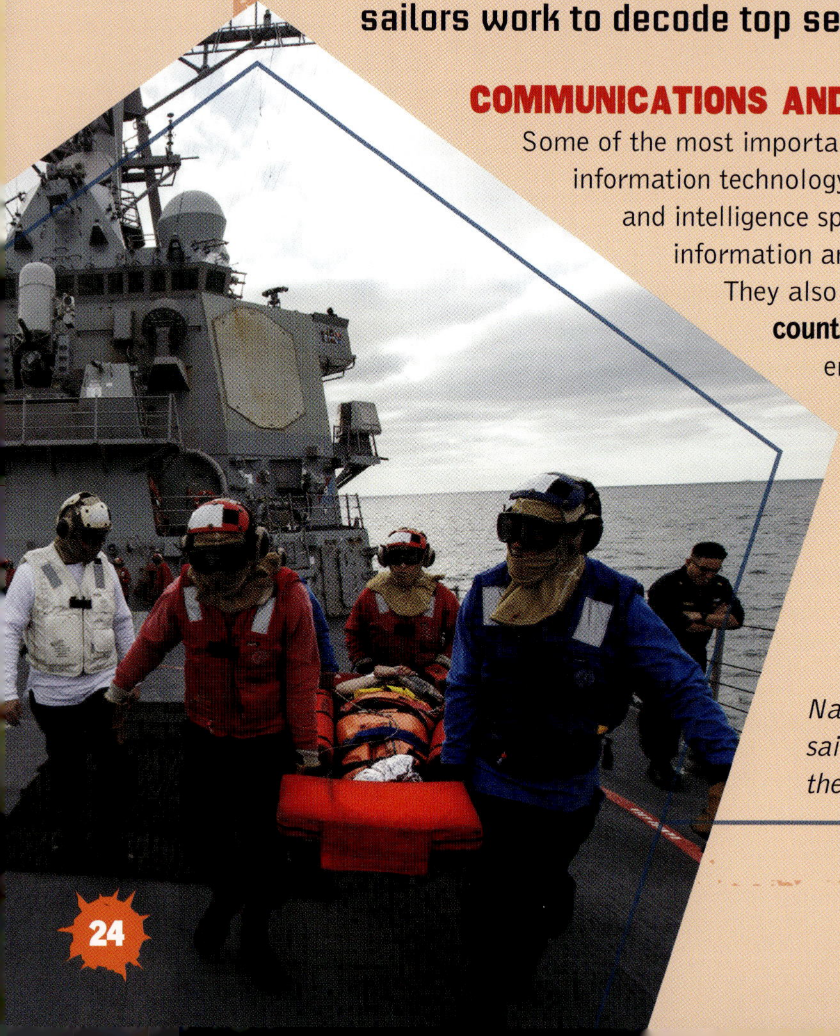

Navy medics transport injured sailors to a safe place where they can then be treated.

Operations specialists work on board ships. Their duties include supplying navigation information, weapons control, and operating surveillance radar.

NUCLEAR POWER EXPERTS

The Navy's nuclear-powered ships, submarines, and weapons need specially trained technicians. Nuclear power technicians serve on board these ships because nuclear power requires a constant watch. Technicians may spend much longer periods at sea than other sailors.

WORKING WITH MACHINES

Many thousands of people work as technicians and engineers on the Navy's warships, submarines, aircraft, and other technologies. These are the people who make sure that all of the Navy's machines and electronics systems are working. For example, aviation mechanics work on some of the most advanced aircraft in the world. Flight operator **personnel** support missions. For example, some flight operators plot aircraft positions and work with pilots to control aircraft systems. Others check equipment or work on charts and maps. The Navy's ships and submarines are large and complicated. They need different specialists to keep them running, such as a Navy submarine electronics technician who works on a submarine's wiring system. Ships have hull maintenance technicians. They are trained to work with different metals and to maintain and repair a ship's structure.

SUPPORT Stories

Leading Seaman Guillaume Durand: SONAR OPERATOR

The ocean is teeming with life, but not all of it is welcoming. An enemy submarine can approach silently, launching torpedoes at lightning speed. Underwater mines lie on the ocean floor, ready to explode a passing naval ship. Sonar operators listen to everything. They find, identify, and track these threats.

Leading Seaman Guillaume Durand is a sonar operator in the Canadian Navy. He is important to any anti-submarine warfare plan, because his skills can be used to defend a Navy fleet or to find and attack enemy vessels.

Durand works on a Canadian Navy surface warship. He spends his days analyzing even the tiniest sounds. His training means that he knows how different sounds travel through water. Is the noise coming from ocean wildlife? Is it a submarine or a warship on the water? The ship and crew's safety depend on Durand knowing the difference.

Durand has studied the sounds that ships and submarines might make. He also has a good understanding of oceanography, the science that studies the ocean. He never talks about the details of his work because anti-submarine warfare plans are top secret. However, we do know that the job involves passive and active sonar equipment.

Your FRONTLINE Career

Is Being a Sonar Operator for You?

Sounds Great

- Working with state-of-the-art equipment
- Being the first to detect important information
- Taking part in secret intelligence-gathering operations
- Being part of important rescue and emergency missions

Things to Think About

- Must be prepared to spend much of the time aboard a ship
- May work on a surface ship or submarine
- Should be very patient and enjoy analyzing information
- Working in a small space

Passive sonar uses hydrophones, or underwater microphones. The hydrophones pick up sounds and change them into electrical signals. Durand listens to the sounds and looks at the signals on his computer. This kind of sonar is best for secret missions. It allows the Navy to detect enemy vessels without revealing its own position.

Sometimes, objects are too quiet for passive sonar to detect. Underwater mines, for example, are still and silent. In such cases, the Navy may use active sonar, which works by sending out pulses of sound through the water. The pulses, or pings, reflect off any object they find and send the information back.

Durand's work is exciting and challenging. More than once, he has been called to "action stations." This is the call that tells the crew to be ready for combat. During peacetime, Durand takes part in simulated battle situations. This is good training for the real thing. To do the job well, Durand has to be focused and pay attention to detail. He is a good problem solver and a quick thinker. These skills help him protect his ship and crew at all times.

Sonar operators check and use sonobuoys. These are devices that are dropped into the ocean and use sound to locate and identify targets.

COULD YOU BE ON THE FRONT LINE?

Do you have what it takes to be in the Navy? Here are some of the key things to think about if you want a career at sea.

EDUCATION

To get into the U.S. or Canadian Navy, you need a high school diploma or GED. You can take courses in school to help you in your career. For example, science courses, including computing or technology classes, may be useful. If you want to be an officer, you must have a university or college degree and have officer training.

FAMILY

Talk to your family about why you want to join the Navy. Be aware that the Navy takes you away from home. Ships may be at sea for two weeks each month. You may be on a mission for six months, staying at foreign bases.

FITNESS

You have to be physically fit to join the Navy. Before applying, make sure you are exercising and eating well. You must be able to swim. The Navy will test your fitness and your swimming. Sign up for team sports. This will keep you moving and develop your team skills. In the Navy, everyone works as a team.

DISCIPLINE

The Navy has high standards of discipline. It expects sailors to follow orders to be ready for action at any time. Learn to keep your bedroom and clothes clean and tidy. Keep your schoolwork organized.

COMMITMENT, HONOR, AND COURAGE

Joining the Navy means that you stay true to the three core values. Commitment means being prepared for tough training. You cannot give up, even when you feel mentally or physically tired. You also have to have a commitment to your fellow sailors. At all times, you must be honest, loyal, and brave.

CARVING A CAREER

There are many different opportunities in the U.S. and Canadian navies. Find out about them, and think about what you might like to do.

LEARN MORE

To find out more about life in the Navy and what it offers, go online (see links on page 31) or contact a local Navy recruiter. A recruiter will be able to answer all your questions.

GLOSSARY

Afghanistan War The war fought by the United States against Taliban forces in Afghanistan
allied Countries or groups that agree to work together
amphibious Describes something that is able to be used on both land and water
aptitude To have a natural ability to do something
ballistic missile A rocket-propelled weapon that shoots through the sky and at long distances before exploding
base A military facility
biological Describes germ warfare, which is a system of using deadly bacteria and viruses to attack people
boot camp A place where newly enlisted people get their basic training
classified Describes top secret information that is known by only a few people
commissioned Appointed or assigned
counterintelligence Keeping the enemy from discovering military or government secrets
covert Secret or hidden
cruise missiles Low-flying weapons that travel at long distances before exploding
cryptologic Describes the study or use of codes
debris Scattered pieces of something left behind
deployed Sent on a mission or tour of duty
enlisting Enrolling in the military
fertilizers Materials that help crops grow
fleets Groups of military ships
guided missile A missile whose course can be changed during its flight, such as with radar
hulls The decks, sides, and bottoms of ships
infantry Military forces that fight on foot
intelligence Secret information
intercepting Preventing something from reaching its intended destination
Marines Soldiers trained to fight on land and sea
mines Explosive devices buried underground
natural disasters Events caused by extreme weather, such as floods and hurricanes, in which people are left homeless and without food and water
navigation To find one's way from one place to another, especially in unknown areas
nuclear powered Describes something that runs on nuclear fuel, which comes from the energy released when atoms are split
offensive On the attack rather than defending a position
personnel The people who work for an organization or company
radar A device that can pick up the position of a person or object using radio waves
reconnaissance To secretly find out about enemy territory
recruiters Military personnel who help people enlist in the armed forces
refugees People forced to leave a country because of war or other reasons
salvage To save something from a wreck
security Protection against enemy danger or threat
siege A situation in which forces surround a place in order to take over and control it
simulation Something made to look or behave like something else
sonar Device using sound waves to find objects underwater
stationed Sent or based, where soldiers stay when they are in battle
stealth A quiet and secretive way to behave
surveillance Watching someone or something to prevent an attack
torpedoes Bombs that are shaped like tubes and explode underwater
values The rules or standards that set the way you behave and treat others every day
Viet Cong A rebel force in South Vietnam that fought with the North Vietnamese
Vietnam War The war fought from 1954 to 1975 between North and South Vietnam. The United States fought on the side of the South Vietnamese.

LEARNING MORE

Discover more about the Navy and careers on the front line.

BOOKS

Boutland, Craig. *Attack Vehicles at Sea: Ships, Submarines, and Patrol Boats* (Military Machines in the War on Terrorism). Capstone Press, 2019.

Reeves, Diane Lindsey. *Military* (Choose Your Own Career Adventure). Cherry Lake Publishing, 2016.

Russo, Kristin J. *Surprising Facts about Being a Navy Sailor.* Edge Books, 2019.

Sneddon, Robert. *The Navy* (Defend and Protect). Gareth Stevens, 2016.

Jeffrey, Gary Spender. *The Vietnam War* (Graphic Modern History: Cold War Conflicts). Crabtree Publishing, 2013.

WEBSITES

The U.S. Navy's site has information about naval careers and what training is needed. Learn what it takes at:
www.navy.com/careers

For information about U.S. Navy careers, education, and training, and information for parents, see:
www.todaysmilitary.com/about-military/service-branches/navy

To join the Canadian Navy, you need to be a Canadian citizen and must be 17 years old (with parental consent) or 18 years old. Find out more at:
https://forces.ca/en/how-to-join

To learn more about Canadian military careers, visit:
https://forces.ca/en/careers

There are specialist training programs for Indigenous peoples in Canada. Learn more at:
https://forces.ca/en/programs-for-indigenous-peoples/#cfaept

INDEX

ABOUT THE AUTHOR

Cynthia O'Brien has written books on careers, history, science, animals, and many other subjects. She found writing about careers in the Navy fascinating, especially learning about how many different, exciting opportunities exist within this service.